John Henry

Tale retold by Bill Balcziak
Illustrated by Drew Rose

Adviser: Dr. Alexa Sandmann, Professor of Literacy,
The University of Toledo; Member, International Reading Association

 COMPASS POINT BOOKS
Minneapolis, Minnesota

Compass Point Books
3109 West 50th Street, #115
Minneapolis, MN 55410

Visit Compass Point Books on the Internet at *www.compasspointbooks.com*
or e-mail your request to *custserv@compasspointbooks.com*

Photographs ©: Carla A. Leslie, 28, 29.

Editor: Catherine Neitge
Designer: Les Tranby

Library of Congress Cataloging-in-Publication Data
Balcziak, Bill, 1962-
  John Henry / written by Bill Balcziak ; illustrated by Drew Rose.
     p. cm. — (The Imagination Series: Tall tales)
Summary: Presents the life story of John Henry, the African American railroad legend known as the "Steel
Driving Man."
  ISBN 0-7565-0457-0 (hardcover)
  1. John Henry (Legendary character)—Legends. [1. John Henry (Legendary character)—Legends. 2. African
Americans—Folklore. 3. Folklore—United States. 4. Tall tales.] I. Title. II. Series.
  PZ8.1.B183 Jo 2003
  398.2'097302—dc21   2002015116

Table of Contents

Man Versus Machine

The tunnel was dark. Dirt and rocks were flying everywhere. John Henry couldn't see. All he could hear was a terrible roar. Sweat was dripping down his face, stinging his eyes.

Noise from the huge machine next to him was so loud it made his teeth hurt. Of course, the heat was terrible, too. Steam covered John like a hot, wet blanket. He felt like he was slowly roasting in an oven.

John paused for a minute and peeled off his wet shirt. His body was soaked in sweat. He was having trouble breathing.

"I can't do this!" John gasped.

A hundred men were watching him from the tunnel entrance. When he stopped, they began chanting, "Go, John, go!" The giant man bent over to catch his breath. A shock of brown hair suddenly appeared at his side. The foreman's son handed John a ladle of water. He looked up at John and said, "You can do it, John Henry!" John thanked him and gave him a tired smile.

The water gave John strength. He lifted his head and stared hard at the steam drill.

"I can beat you," he said. The machine kept drilling.

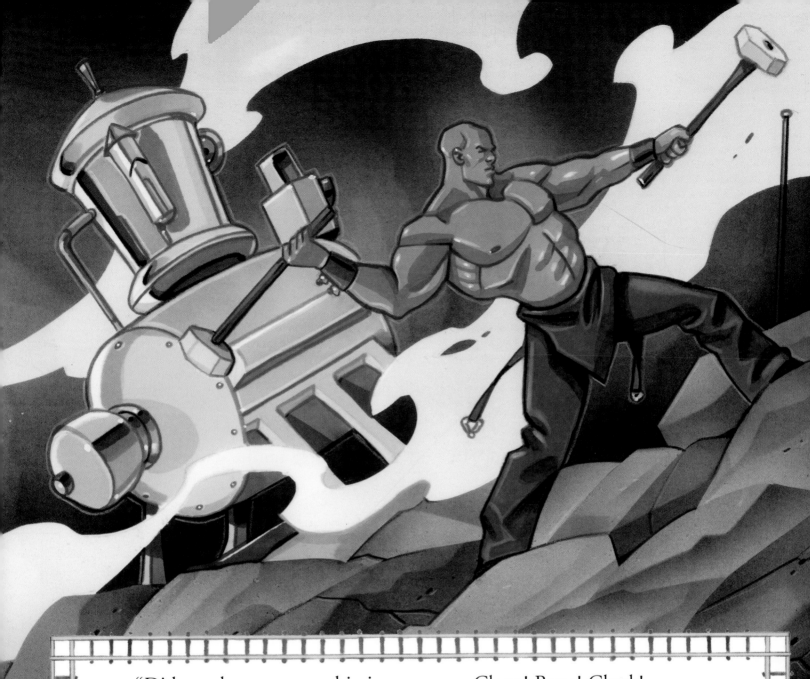

"Did you hear me, you big iron heap? I WILL beat you!" The machine kept hammering.

"I WILL beat you!" The machine kept pounding. "I WILL BEAT YOU!"

John picked up his hammers and started again.

Clang! Bang! Clank!

Clang! Bang! Clank!

Faster and faster he went until the crowd could hardly tell man from machine.

Clang, bang, clank!

Clang, bang, clank!

7

Life as a Slave

John Henry's story began in Virginia before the Civil War. John was born a slave. His mother and father were slaves, too. They were all treated as property. Slaves were forced to work against their will. They got no money. They owned nothing.

As a child, John was expected to work in the fields with his parents as they picked cotton, peanuts, or tobacco. The work was terrible. The days were long in the heat and dust. It was this hard life that shaped John, making him strong and tough.

John was big, too. Some said he grew to be the biggest young man in the South. He stood a head taller than his father and had to duck down low when he went through a doorway. (His shoulders were so broad he had to squeeze through sideways!)

Despite the awful living conditions, John tried to be happy. He dearly loved his friends and family, and they loved him.

Every night after dinner, his tired mother never failed to sing him songs of hope and faith while he fell asleep. And John never failed to dream of freedom. Oh, how he wanted to be free!

One day when he was a young man, John stood with a group of workers near an old barn. The building was leaning down on one side. A foreman was trying to figure out how to raise it up so a support could be placed underneath.

"I can do it," said John Henry from the rear of the group.

"That's impossible," said the foreman. "These ten men can't move it an inch."

John smiled and said, "Just give me a chance, boss." The foreman nodded and stepped aside. John slid his big hands under the corner of the barn. He started to lift. At first, nothing happened. His muscles bulged, and his legs trembled a little.

Then, with a loud groan from the faded walls, the barn slowly began to rise. The men stood with their mouths hanging wide open.

The foreman yelled, "Move those timbers under the barn!" John held the end of the barn up until the men could follow the foreman's order. When they finished, he eased the barn onto the logs and wiped his brow. The foreman couldn't believe it. "That was the most amazing thing I've ever seen," he said.

That's how John Henry became famous. No man could pull, lift, cut, chop, hammer, saw, pound, run, or push like the gentle giant from Virginia. Word spread from one farm to another like a summer storm. The legend of John Henry was born.

Freedom at Last!

The Civil War had torn the country apart. It had pitted the North against the South, freedom against slavery. It finally ended in 1865 after four long, bloody years of fighting.

John and the other slaves were finally free. John left the farm to start a new life. In a nearby town, he saw a group of former slaves gathered at the train station. They were standing near a sign that read:

Wanted:
Men to build the
Chesapeake & Ohio RR.
Good wages.
Meals provided.
Hard work.

John decided to join the group and find a job on the C&O Railroad. He boarded a sleek, shiny train bound for the work camps. The train raced through Virginia and chugged up the Blue Ridge Mountains into West Virginia.

They rode all night and stopped just as the sun was coming up. John got off the train and followed the crowd of men to the camp. They were high in the Allegheny Mountains, surrounded by the biggest hills John had ever seen. The air was cool and smelled of pine and dew.

"This way, men!" yelled a kind-looking man. "This way to the work site!"

When John got there, he couldn't believe his eyes. There were hundreds of tents and thousands of men! He walked up to a tent and peeked inside. Three men sat on cots eating breakfast.

"My, that smells good!" said John.

"Won't you join us, friend?" asked one of the men.

John sat down and asked the men dozens of questions about working on the C&O Railroad. He learned about laying track and drilling tunnels. The men told him how to drive steel and what each man's job was.

In order to build a tunnel, one of the men explained, the workers drilled holes in the rock. Dynamite was packed into the holes and exploded. This explosion blew apart the rock, and the new hole formed another section of tunnel.

Two-man teams did the drilling. One man was the shaker. He held a steel rod in place. The other man was the driver. His job was to pound the rod with a big hammer. John's new friends all agreed that with his size and strength, he would be a great steel driver.

A Two-Hammer Man

The next morning, John followed his new friends out to the work site. The foreman handed John Henry a 10-pound (4.5-kilogram) hammer. He pointed to a tunnel being cored out of the hillside.

"But, boss," John said, "I need a bigger hammer. No, I need TWO hammers!"

The foreman looked at John more closely. He saw John's huge arms and chest. He said, "Yeah, son, you're a two-hammer man if I've ever seen one! Go see the blacksmith."

The blacksmith made John a pair of 40-pound (18-kilogram) hammers. He handed them over with a look of doubt. John sized them up, thanked the man, and was soon pounding his way through the tunnel's rock wall.

Clang, bang, clank went his hammers.

Clang, bang, clank!

John worked as fast as three men, maybe more. His friends watched in wonder. When a man stopped to rest, John doubled his speed to make up lost time.

Clang, bang, clank!

The foreman knew John was the best steel driver who ever lived.

"John," he said, "you're going to die with a hammer in your hand."

18

One day, a salesman led a team of horses up the road to the work site. The horses were hauling a giant machine called a steam drill.

"Hold it right there!" said the foreman waving his arms. "We don't need that thing. Look at these men! This is the best steel driving crew in the entire world!"

The salesman smiled and took the foreman aside. "Maybe so, my friend. But nothing is faster than this machine. It will outwork twenty men, and it never stops to rest." The salesman offered to prove his claim.

The foreman took off his cap and scratched his head. He watched John Henry pounding away nearby and told the salesman he would make him a deal. If the steam drill could beat John in a steel driving competition the next day, he would buy ten new machines.

Race to the Finish

"You're on!" said the salesman. The next morning John Henry ate a huge breakfast and marched to the work site. A crowd of men already circled the steam drill, watching it chug away in the deep, dark tunnel. It steamed and hissed and banged and screeched.

John paid no attention to it. He lifted his hammers and looked at the foreman.

"Ready, boss!" he cried. The foreman nodded at John.

"First one through the mountain to the other side wins the race!" he shouted above the noise of the steam drill. The salesman and his helpers shoved the machine up to the rock wall, and the race began!

The steam drill exploded into action. Its long steel rod blasted into the rock, spraying stones at the crowd. They gasped at the speed of the drill. It was way ahead of John!

Clang, bang, clank went John's hammers. He kept a steady pace, but he couldn't keep up.

John stopped to take a drink from the foreman's son. The water gave him a second wind, and he doubled his pace.

Clang, bang, clank!

Sure enough, he was catching up to the drill! The men cheered even louder for John.

Clang, bang, clank!

After six hours, John was even with the steam drill. After eight hours, he was slightly ahead. At twelve hours, John began to tire and fall behind. The foreman walked over and ordered John to stop. "That's enough, John. You've done more than any man could have dreamed."

John wasn't listening. He looked back at the foreman and smiled.

"I'm OK, boss. Just watch me now!" John worked faster and faster. Sparks flew from the hammers as they hit steel. Bang, bang, bang, bang, bang, bang, bang went the hammers. The rock all but melted under John's blows.

Suddenly, there was a change in the sound inside the tunnel. The steam drill had stopped! Oil and water poured from the engine as the steam drill gasped its last breath. The machine was dead.

John slowly lowered his hammers. He walked to the tunnel entrance and drew in deep breaths of cool, clean air. He smiled at the men and shook their hands. "See," he said. "I told you I would beat that old iron heap." Then the big man lay down on the ground, closed his eyes, and gasped his last breath.

John Henry was dead.

24

That night, the tearful men laid John Henry
to rest. And they sang:

Listen to my story;
'Tis a story true;
About a mighty man,
John Henry was his name.
And John Henry was a steel driver, too.
Lord, Lord,
John Henry was a steel driver, too.

Soon, the other men sang along:
John Henry had a hammer;
Weighed nigh forty pound;
Every time John made a strike
He seen his steel go 'bout two inches down.
Lord, Lord,
He seen his steel go 'bout two inches down.

When the song was done, the men heard the low
rumble of thunder from a faraway summer storm. They
turned to each other and smiled. That sound, they said, was
John Henry's mighty hammers pounding their eternal beat.

The Life of John Henry

John Henry grows up in slavery.

John Henry uses his strength to help the foreman.

John Henry arrives at the C&O work camp.

John Henry works on the C&O railroad.

John Henry races the steam drill to the end.

Pennsylvania

Maryland

West Virginia

Virginia

North Carolina

South Carolina

The legend of John Henry goes back more than 130 years. It started with the miners drilling the Big Bend Tunnel of the Chesapeake and Ohio Railroad in West Virginia.

This story of man versus machine might be based on a real person, but we'll never know for sure. We do know, however, that the story of John Henry is one of America's most loved tall tales. It has even inspired many songs, including the most popular folk song of all time, "John Henry."

Although he is usually thought of as African-American, some stories say John Henry is white or Asian or Hispanic. He is many things to many people. Most importantly, however, John Henry is one of America's greatest symbols of strength and pride.

28

Southern Cornbread

Here is a recipe for real Southern cornbread. The men working on the C&O Railroad would have loved it! Did you know there is a huge difference between the cornbread recipes found in the North and South? In the North, cooks use quite a bit of sugar and flour in their cornbread. In the South, cooks use little if any sugar and flour. But, my, is it good!

1 cup buttermilk
1 cup stone ground cornmeal
1 teaspoon salt

1/2 teaspoon baking soda
1 egg
1 tablespoon shortening

Preheat oven to 450 degrees F. Melt the shortening in a 9-inch round iron skillet in the oven. Stir the cornmeal, salt, and baking soda together. Add the egg and buttermilk and mix well. Have an adult help you remove the hot skillet from the oven. Pour the batter into the skillet, stirring the melted shortening into the batter. Bake at 450 degrees for 30 to 40 minutes. Remove from oven when top of cornbread is brown. Put the cornbread on a serving plate and cut into wedges. Serve right away with butter.

Glossary

Allegheny and Blue Ridge Mountains—ranges of the Appalachian mountain system that run through the eastern states from Pennsylvania to Georgia

amazing—surprising

competition—a contest

dynamite—an explosive used to make tunnels

foreman—the boss

legend—a story passed down through the years that may not be completely true

Statue of John Henry in Talcott, West Virginia

Did You Know?

➤ More Americans died in the Civil War than in any other war. It was fought from 1861 to 1865 between the Northern states and the Southern states. When it was over, the Union was saved and slavery ended.

➤ In the 1920s, Guy B. Johnson of the University of North Carolina wrote books about John Henry and Southern folk songs. He made the first real effort to track down the legends, traditions, and songs about the "steel-driving man." The song lyrics on page 26 were taken from a version sung by construction workers in Alabama in the early 1900s.

➤ There is an 8-foot (2.4 m) bronze statue of John Henry near Big Bend Tunnel in Talcott, West Virginia.

➤ "John Henry" is the most recorded folk song in the United States.

➤ John Henry appeared on a 32-cent United States postage stamp in 1996.

Want to Know More?

At the Library

Keats, Ezra Jack. *John Henry: An American Legend.* New York: Knopf, 1987.

Lester, Julius, and Jerry Pinkney. *John Henry.* New York: Dial Books, 1994.

Jensen, Patsy, and Roseanne Litzinger. *John Henry and His Mighty Hammer.* New York: Troll Communications, 1997.

Walker, Paul Robert. *Big Men, Big Country: A Collection of American Tall Tales.* New York: Harcourt, 1999.

On the Web

Jump Back in Time

http://www.americaslibrary.gov/ cgi-bin/page.cgi/jb
To learn about the Civil War and Reconstruction, which is the name of the period that followed the war

Cultural Arts Resources for Teachers and Students

http://www.carts.org/carts_artist4.html
To listen to blues singer John Cephas sing the ballad "John Henry"

Through the Mail

B&O Railroad Museum

901 W. Pratt St.
Baltimore, MD 21223
410/752-2490
For information on the B&O Railroad Museum's 175th anniversary celebration and the World's Festival of Trains

On the Road

John Henry Days Festival

Summers County Convention & Visitors Bureau
206 Temple Street
Hinton, West Virginia 25951
To attend this yearly festival held each July at the Big Bend Tunnel in Talcott, West Virginia

A historical marker, entitled "Big Bend Tunnel," stands near the tunnel entrance in Talcott, West Virginia. It says: The great tunnel of the C&O Railroad was started at Big Bend in 1870, and completed three years later. It is more than a mile long, and now has a twin tunnel. Tradition makes this the scene of the steel drivers' ballad, "John Henry."

Index

About the Author

Bill Balcziak has written a number of books for children. When he is not writing, he enjoys going to plays, movies, and museums. Bill lives in Minnesota with his family under the shadow of Paul Bunyan and Babe, the Blue Ox.

About the Illustrator

Drew Rose spent many afternoons of his childhood enjoying the illustrations in books at the library. Now he is happy to help other stories come to life with his own art. His wife, Tricia, and their two cats, Iris and Micetro, live with him in Atlanta, Georgia.